THE GRAND WoLF

Avril McDonald

Illustrated by Tatiana Minina

Crown House Publishing Limited
www.crownhouse.co.uk

First published by

Crown House Publishing Ltd
Crown Buildings, Bancyfelin, Carmarthen, Wales, SA33 5ND, UK
www.crownhouse.co.uk

and

Crown House Publishing Company LLC
6 Trowbridge Drive, Suite 5, Bethel, CT 06801, USA
www.crownhousepublishing.com

Illustrations by Tatiana Minina

British Library Cataloguing-in-Publication Data
A catalogue entry for this book is available from the British Library.

Print ISBN: 978-178583019-8
Mobi ISBN: 978-178583073-0
ePub ISBN: 978-178583074-7
ePDF ISBN: 978-178583075-4

LCCN 2015953331

Printed and bound in the UK by
Gomer Press, Llandysul, Ceredigion

Because the one thing that's true is true love never dies!

Thanks to Åsa Pettersson for her inspiration and contribution to
Feel Brave's work and to the poet Robert Saxton for his editorial directive.

Once in a while,
on a clear sunny day,
Wolfgang would go
to the Grand Wolf's to play.

Across fields of buttercups
just past the trees
Stood his house, among poppies
that laughed in the breeze.

The Grand Wolf was gentle
with kind smiling eyes.

He could swing you so high
that your feet touched the skies.

... Or go for long walks
where he'd talk of great things,

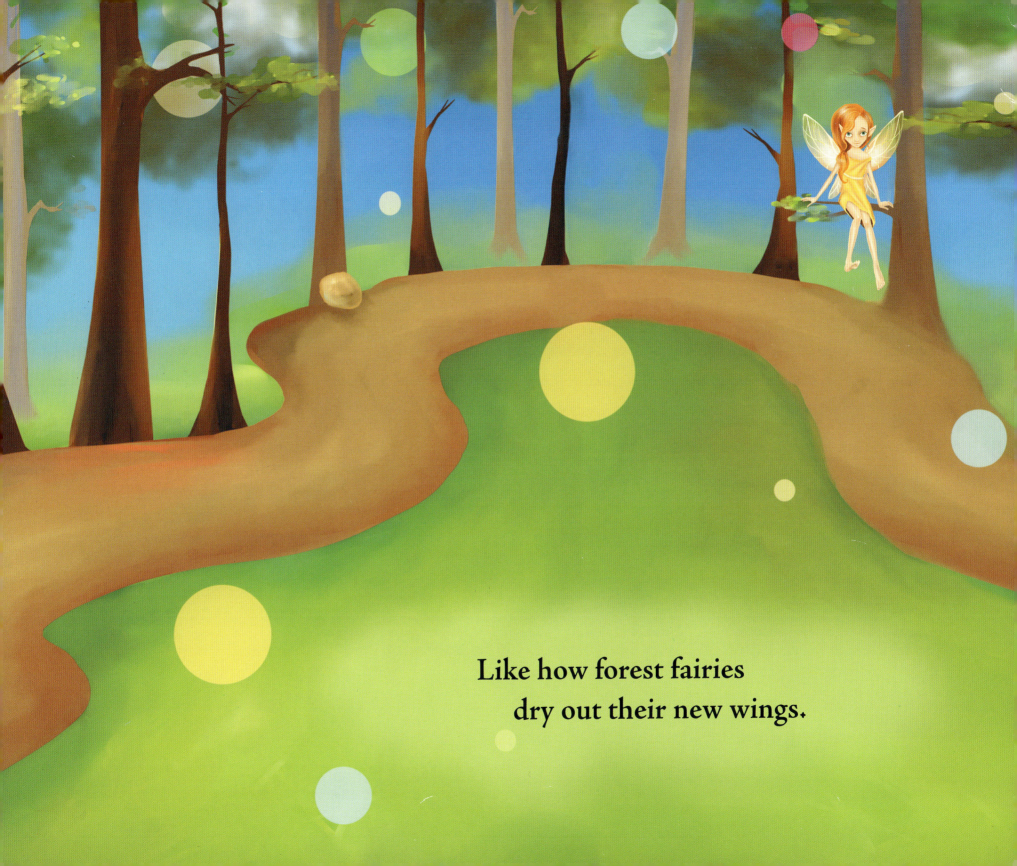

Like how forest fairies
dry out their new wings.

There were frogs in his garden
and toys in his shed.
His kitchen was filled
with the smells of fresh bread.

It was such fun to go there
with so much to do,
And when Wolfgang went over,
his friends all went too.

But one day they got there
and things seemed quite bad.
The sky had turned grey
and the frogs all looked sad.

The pretty bright poppies
were wrinkled and dried.
Then down flew Wise Owl and said,
"Grand Wolf has … died."

"Are you sure?" asked Catreen
as she held back a tear.
"Yes, it's true," said Wise Owl,
"he is no longer here.
His body was old
and a star shining bright
Gently guided him off
in the still of the night.

Just as leaves fall from trees
and the winter brings snow,
We all change.
There's another grand place we all go."

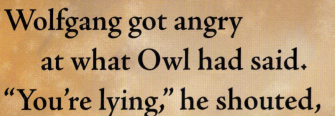

Wolfgang got angry
  at what Owl had said.
"You're lying," he shouted,
  "the Grand Wolf's not dead!

He wouldn't just *leave* us,
  that's not what he'd do.
Look, he's there, in the field!
  I can see him, can't you?"

So they ran to the Grand Wolf
to hear what he'd say.
They couldn't believe
he would leave them that way.

But then as they got closer,
their hearts filled with doubt:
It was just Scarecrow Jack
chasing birds all about.

They could see Scarecrow Jack
had been crying real tears –
Well, Grand Wolf and Jack
had been best friends for years.

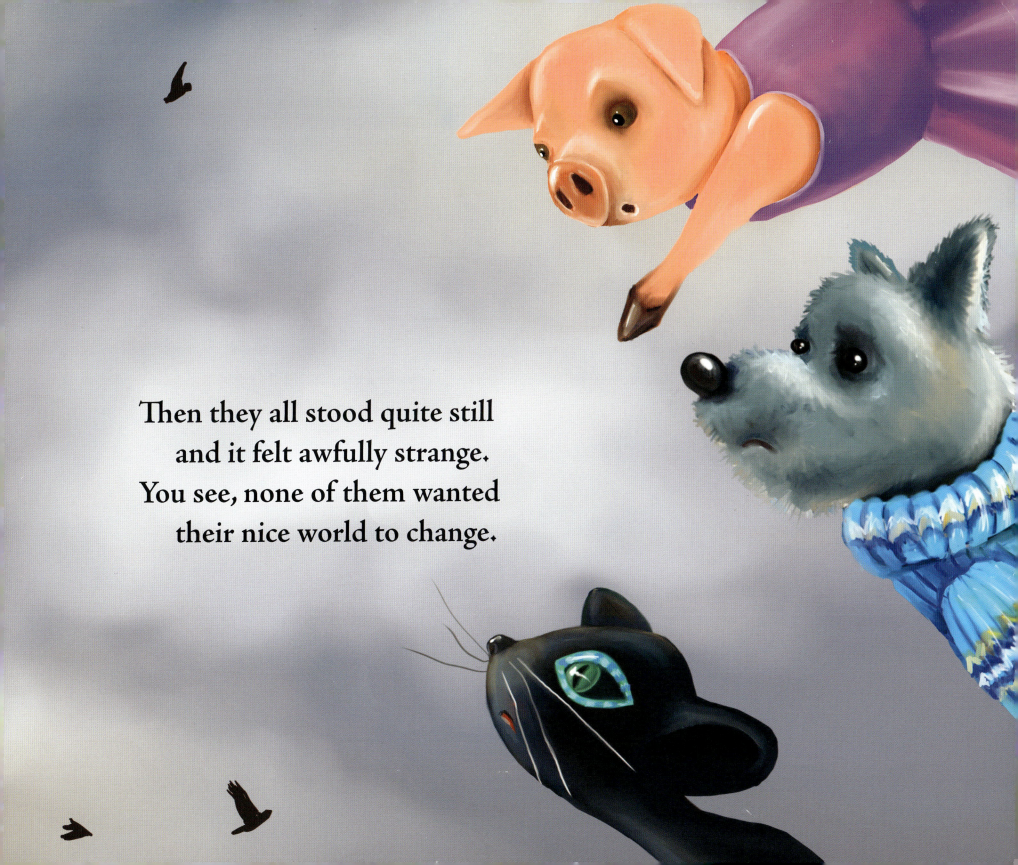

Then they all stood quite still
and it felt awfully strange.
You see, none of them wanted
their nice world to change.

But it did change that day,
Wise Owl hadn't lied.

All the fairies' hearts broke
as they joined them and cried.

As the days and weeks passed,
no one had any fun.

Then Spider crept down
from the web that she'd spun ...

"My dear Wolfgang," said Spider,
　　"it's helpful to cry.
Every tear says 'I love you'
　　that falls from your eye.
But now that he's gone
　　you're not so far apart,
If you just learn to see
　　the Grand Wolf with your heart.

Talk of the good times
   you had and hold dear,
Be still now and then …
   and you might feel him near.
He will always be close,
   we see him in your eyes …
And the one thing that's true
   is true love never dies."

They all put up photos,
which made them feel better,

Wolfgang wrote Grand Wolf
a lovely long letter.

Then one day while playing
with his ship in the shed,
Wolfgang felt Grand Wolf near him
and heard what he said:

"When you play in the forest,
    I'll whisper in streams.
In the night when you're sleeping
    we'll talk in your dreams.
In buttercup fields,
    we'll hold hands as we run.
You'll feel all my love
    from the warmth of the sun.
My voice will go with you,
    like winds in the sky.
I'm here in your heart
    if you'll keep me close by."

Wolfgang felt peaceful
and happy inside.
His heart started glowing
with feelings of pride.

Then he watered the flowers
till a big moon rose bright,
And his friends built a fire
to welcome the night.

They told jokes to the frogs,
which brought their smiles back,
And gave Grand Wolf's best shirt
to old Scarecrow Jack.

Then they danced to remember
the joy of best friends
And to know in their hearts
that true love never ends.